THE FIREMAN

BWWM Romance Series

JAMILA JASPER

Jamila Jasper Romance

Copyright © 2018 by Jamila Jasper

ISBN: 9781717912305

All rights reserved.

No part of this book may be reproduced in any form or by any electronic or mechanical means, including information storage and retrieval systems, without written permission from the author, except for the use of brief quotations in a book review.

❦ Created with Vellum

COMPLETE SERIES

The Pool Boy

The Plumber

The Gardener

The Fireman

The Builder

I
THE FIREMAN

After my conversation with Shontal, I found myself more determined than ever to stick to my vow of celibacy. I had stuck to my vows for over 20 years and as of yet, I saw no reason to break those vows. I had held steadfast for 20 years after all. Now that I was approaching 61, why should I change?

What man could do something for me that I couldn't do for myself? I was the pure definition of an independent woman in every sense of the word.

20 years was a long time to hold true to a value like that. In the world, people expected me to just find a man and settle down. No man had treated me well enough or done enough for me. I loved my cats, but that was about it. A man had never proven himself to me and I had never held that against most men. Men were simply inadequate.

I mean ask yourself... When's the last time you men a strong, strapping man with a good income, no baby mamas and a strong Christian work ethic who liked a real down to earth woman? I struggled to find a man like that since I'd started searching.

I considered myself luckier and luckier the older I got. If the perfect man was going to come along, I could meet him at any time.

I kept my cats organized in the most peculiar way — at least others believed my methods peculiar while I noted their efficacy. Each one of my princes had their very own home outside, their very own water dish, and their very own food dish. Each morning, I would cook up a fresh meal of sausages and other delightful meats for my pets. I treated them as if they were friends. They were friends.

Sometimes, I would even make them creamy coffee which they lapped at with their soft little tongues. In a way, they were my closest friends aside from the girls, Kishawn, Shontal, Ronice and Tasha. The cats were more loyal to me than any man had ever been.

My three favorite cats out of all my collective were named Horace, Homer, and Virgil. All of them were named after Greek writers. I loved reading the classic Greek myths especially the ones involving Zeus and Hera. Reading those myths, I wondered why on earth Hera would ever put up with a husband like that – – a man who cared nothing for her and only cared for getting his own needs met. That was one of the main reasons I was single. I saw the truth in these myths. I saw that most men are just like Zeus. They were only after one thing.

One afternoon, I sat on my porch sipping iced tea and watching as Horace and Homer frolicked in the grass. They enjoy playing with each other in the afternoon and they would race around pouncing on each other and then rolling around into balls of fur until one or the other got the upper hand and sent the other one running along its way. As they were frolicking and fighting, neither cat noticed a truck barreling down the street.

I stood up, clutching my iced tea as droplets of condensation dripped down my palms. my heart thudded in my chest as I anticipated the inevitable.

"Careful!" I screamed.

My voice alarmed the cats just enough for them to break apart and terrified for their lives they separated and fled in opposite directions to escape the oncoming truck.

Horace had crossed the street, but Homer had launched himself up the tall oak tree in my backyard. I shrieked again, this time dropping the iced tea to the ground. The glass didn't shatter but my spilled drink splashed all over my feet.

I didn't care. All I cared about was Homer. In his terror, Homer had climbed so far up the tree but there was no way he could jump down. With my bad hip and arthritis in both my hip and wrist, I had a very slim chance of getting to him myself.

When I was a younger woman, I might have been able to shimmy up the side of the tree and coax Homer to at least jump into my arms. I had plenty of tree climbing days in my youth but those days were behind me. Now, I was an older woman, my sixtieth birthday had been Midsummer. I was fairly powerless to convince the cat to come down on his own. Not even fresh cooked turkey giblets could convince him to leap into the wicker basket I extended to the sky.

Homer let out a pitiful mewling sound. The sound filled me with anguish.

I knew my kitty needed help, but none of her neighbors had returned home from work yet. Even the friendly neighbor boy Nelson Jones had just found himself in employment and would be nowhere nearby to help. I had to do the unthinkable. I had to disrupt our small town's volunteer fire department and get one of these volunteer firemen to mosey on over away to my place just to help me get my cat out of a tree.

I was becoming a stereotypical cat woman and I had no one to blame but myself. For a long time, Tasha and even Ronice warned me that my problem was getting out of control.

Tasha, of course, wasted no time in telling me that I would be single for life if I did not get rid of at least half of these cats. How the heck could I get rid of my friends? They had been reliable and by my side for as long as I could remember. I took care of them as if they were my kids.

And, as I approached 61 and eventually retired, it would be for the best if I kept my friends close.

I hustled inside as fast as my throbbing hip could take me to get to the phone. I have a nonemergency line for the fire department lying around because I'm an older woman and I get a bit paranoid. I had a suspicion something like this could happen at any time and finally, my worst fears had come true. I needed help. And I needed help from a man to make it worse.

Laden with shame, I picked up my phone and dialed the number. I knew most of the volunteer firemen especially the chief who had gone to university with me oh so long ago. His nickname back then had been Turtle, so I still referred to him as such affectionately.

"Turtle! I need your help. My cat is stuck in a tree I can't get him down."

After chortling at my pain, he assured me that he would be sending one of his best men down to help me.

"Who is it?"

I wanted to know exactly which of the guys Turtle planned to send to help me. Not all the volunteer firemen had the same level of skill and talent. Some of the younger ones were particularly lazy. When Ronice had a small fire at her backyard barbecue the previous year, they'd taken a full forty-five minutes to show up!

"I'm sending the best, trust me."

Turtle hung up and I realized that I really did have no choice but to trust him. I hastened over to the oak tree and cooed to Homer, promising that very soon someone would be on their way to help set him free.

Meow!

Some response. He didn't seem too comforted by my promise of the fireman on his way would be one of the best (if Turtle) were to be believed.

I waited agitated at the end of my driveway for some sign that a volunteer fireman would eventually show up. Didn't Turtle realize how important this was to me? After a long ten minutes that seemed to stretch out for eons, a forest green Dodge pickup truck pulled down my cul-de-sac and parked in front of my driveway.

A man that I did not recognize jumped out. He had short black hair and dark brown eyes, with deeply tanned skin. I ascertained he was a fireman only by the sticker on his car. He walked towards me with a scowl on his face.

"Are you Mrs. Zelda?"

"Just Zelda, thank you."

He grunted.

How rude! I thought to myself.

"Good morning Sir," I said pointedly, hoping I could point out to this useful and arrogant fireman good manners never killed anybody.

"It was a good morning. Mind telling me what the problem is?"

His frustration agitated me.

Now I hate a man with a bad attitude. I'm sorry, it's just not something I can stand. I could tell this fireman needed an attitude adjustment. If he didn't fix his act up, I'd get Turtle back on the line pronto.

"No. I'm not going to tell you what the problem is until I find out your name.

He grunted again. But this time, he had the good sense to tell me his name afterward.

"The names Lance. Lance Lumber."

Lance Lumber? I didn't remember hearing that name before. In fact, I didn't recognize the name at all. He must have been new in town. Maybe that or I just didn't know many men so many years younger than me. Lance Lumber couldn't have been a day over 35. He had a sharp angular face and thick arms that bulged from his shirt like tree trunks.

"Are you new?" I asked in disbelief. I had a hard time believing that a volunteer fireman would have such a bad attitude. What on earth was wrong with this guy?

"Not new. Just busy. Busy and tired of civilians calling us firemen for nonsense."

"It's not nonsense! My cat is stuck in that tree. Now you get him down right this instant!"

I was not usually the sort of woman who got angry or raised her voice. But when it came to my cats, I was as protective as a mama bear. I refused to let Lance Lumber get away with acting like Homer's plight was unimportant. He was a volunteer fireman after all. This was his job -- by choice!

I was ready to tear into him but I noticed his response to my comment. His nose wrinkled and he unfolded his arms, relaxing just a bit.

"Wait. This isn't a burned popcorn house?" "

"No! My cat is stuck in a tree and I need your help getting it down."

His expression softened.

"My apologies, Zelda. I've had a number of false alarms this week and Turtle keeps sending me to deal with these damn teens who won't stop burning popcorn and activating their systems. I thought this was another incident.

"Is that why I got all that bad attitude?"

"Again, my apologies. If there's any way I could make it up

JAMILA JASPER

to you..."

"Just get my cat down!"

"As you wish ma'am."

Lance asked me to direct him to the tree, which I did.

I approached the base of my oak tree and my eyes traveled all the way up to where my beautiful cat sat crouched between a branch and the tree trunk, shaking in terror.

"The little guy looks scared. What's his name?"

"This is Homer. I've got other cats too. But he's one of the weakest. And the dumbest."

Lance chuckled.

"What do you know? I love cats. The dumber the better."

He flashed a smile for the first time I noticed that Lance Lumber was not an unattractive man. Sure, he was more than 20 years my junior. That made him off-limits even if I would have ever considered breaking my vow of celibacy.

But when you're like me and you venture into a vow of celibacy, it does not hurt to look. And believe me, I looked. Lance eyed the height of the tree and determined that he would have no choice but to climb up himself. My tree grew in such a strange way that he could not fix a ladder against it safely. The ground at the base was uneven to boot -- a problem caused by my former gardener, Kai Lord.

I cautioned him, warning Lance, letting him know that I did not want to be liable if he were to fall and crack his neck.

"Don't worry. I like a challenge."

I had no choice but to trust him. If he thought he could climb that tree and get my cat down and if Turtle had said he was the very best, all I could do was hope that neither of them had been exaggerating their talents and my kitty would soon be home safe.

"Don't say I didn't warn you."

Lance eyed the tree, determining the best path up.

"Hot today, ain't it?" He said.

"Yes," I replied.

I was in no mood for small talk. Homer let out a whimpering meow that didn't just tug at my heartstrings — it yanked. I just wanted Lance to hurry up and bring him home without any further muss or fuss.

"I don't think I can make it up there with this shirt on…"

Before I could protest, Lance reached for the base of his white shirt and stripped it off, exposing his bare fireman's chest. My hand clasped to my mouth. Had this man essentially disrobed before me?! Before he could turn around and notice the look of shock on my face, I composed myself. He'd already worked up a sweat. Every inch of his thick sinewy body was covered in muscle. He had a few tattoos of birds traveling up the left side of his body. His abs pulsed in the midday sun.

He raised his hand to cover his eyes as he stared up the tree.

"I'll wrap this shirt around him to get him down. Shouldn't be a problem."
"Are you sure?!"

"Yeah, I'm sure."

His confidence impressed me. In a matter of a few minutes, Lance had assuaged my concerns. I can't help but be mesmerized by a man of action.

Before I could protest, Lance began to shimmy up the side of the tree. He hoisted his thick body up as if it were weightless. Grasping one thin branch, he swung his body up to a thicker one that was more certain to hold his weight.

"Be careful!" I called up to him.

Lance grunted in response. Homer let out another anguished meow. I rushed to the base of the tree, tilting my head up towards the canopy of leaves, hoping to make out exactly where my silly cat had stuck.

"I got it!" he called back.

He climbed even higher, near the top of the oak tree. From the ground, he looked so small but I'd seen his muscles and knew he had the strength to pull himself up and get down. I trusted that he'd save Homer. I didn't have much of a choice but to trust him.

He'd gone so far up that I couldn't make him out. The sun blinded me and all I could do was listen to the rustling of leaves, Homer's occasional meow, and Lance's grunts as he climbed higher and higher.

I heard a loud yowl and then Lance called down to me, "I got him!"

"Is he okay?"

"A bit shook up but he'll be fine!"

Lance scooped Homer under his arm, wrapping him in a shirt so his sharp claws couldn't dig into his flesh. He descended cautiously, using his one free hand to balance himself as he stepped from branch to branch. About eight feet from the bottom of the tree, Lance sat on the branch and leaned down.

"Come get him."

"Mama's coming Homer!" I called, running to Lance's position and grabbing the cat from his hands, holding him close.

Despite the comfort of my affection, Homer still longed for his paws to touch the ground. He wriggled out of my arms and darted off towards Virgil who sat on the porch with a disapproving gaze plastered on his furry white face.

Lance chuckled.

THE FIREMAN

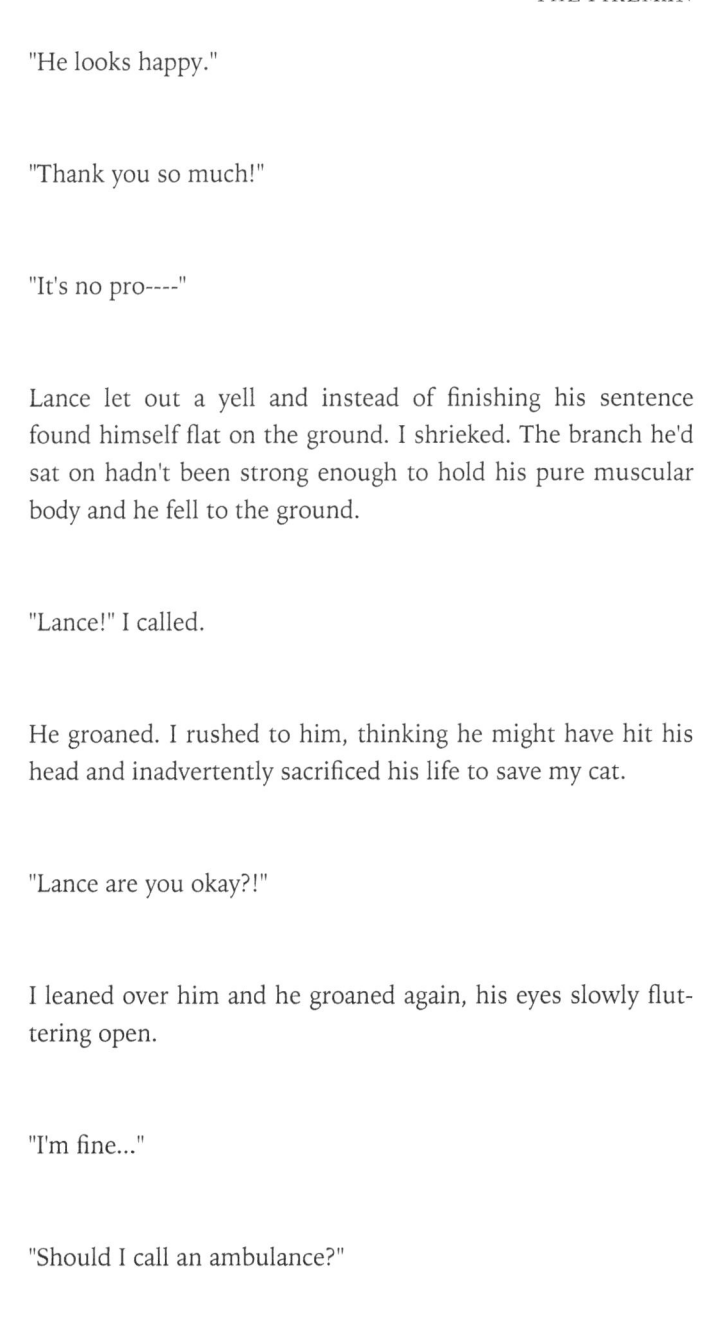

"He looks happy."

"Thank you so much!"

"It's no pro----"

Lance let out a yell and instead of finishing his sentence found himself flat on the ground. I shrieked. The branch he'd sat on hadn't been strong enough to hold his pure muscular body and he fell to the ground.

"Lance!" I called.

He groaned. I rushed to him, thinking he might have hit his head and inadvertently sacrificed his life to save my cat.

"Lance are you okay?!"

I leaned over him and he groaned again, his eyes slowly fluttering open.

"I'm fine..."

"Should I call an ambulance?"

15

JAMILA JASPER

"No!"

He sat up and blood gushed from a large scrape on his back.

"You're hurt!"

"I'm fine..."

"I can't let you leave here like this! Turtle would never send another guy here to help me."

He grunted.

"Stand up, I insist you come inside this instant!"

Lance raised his eyebrows but he didn't protest. That's right. One thing about us older black women is we know how to command respect. He brushed his jeans off and grumbled, "Okay, I'll come inside. I just need a band-aid."

"A band-aid? Mr. Lumber, your back is scraped up nearly to oblivion. You need more than a band-aid. You need this wound to get cleaned up and you need some gauze on it."

"You can do all that?"

"I'm a nurse! Of course, I can."

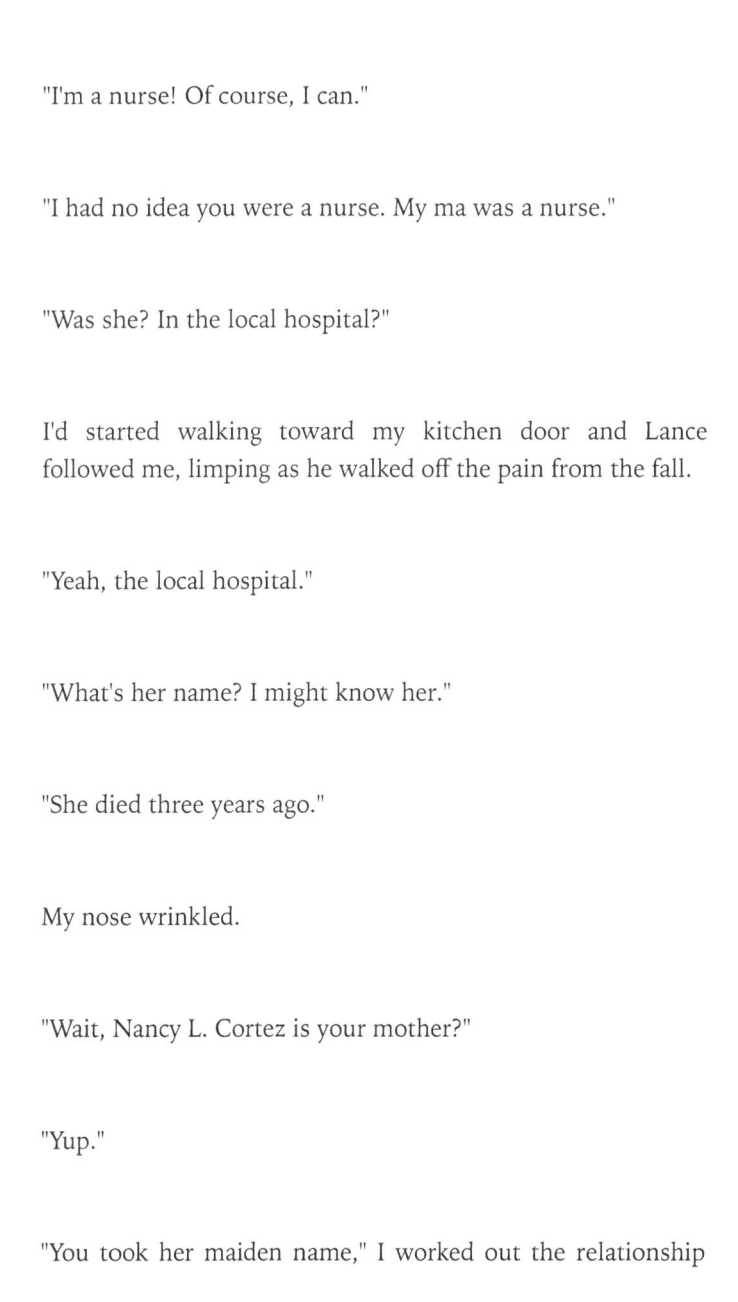

"I had no idea you were a nurse. My ma was a nurse."

"Was she? In the local hospital?"

I'd started walking toward my kitchen door and Lance followed me, limping as he walked off the pain from the fall.

"Yeah, the local hospital."

"What's her name? I might know her."

"She died three years ago."

My nose wrinkled.

"Wait, Nancy L. Cortez is your mother?"

"Yup."

"You took her maiden name," I worked out the relationship

out loud.

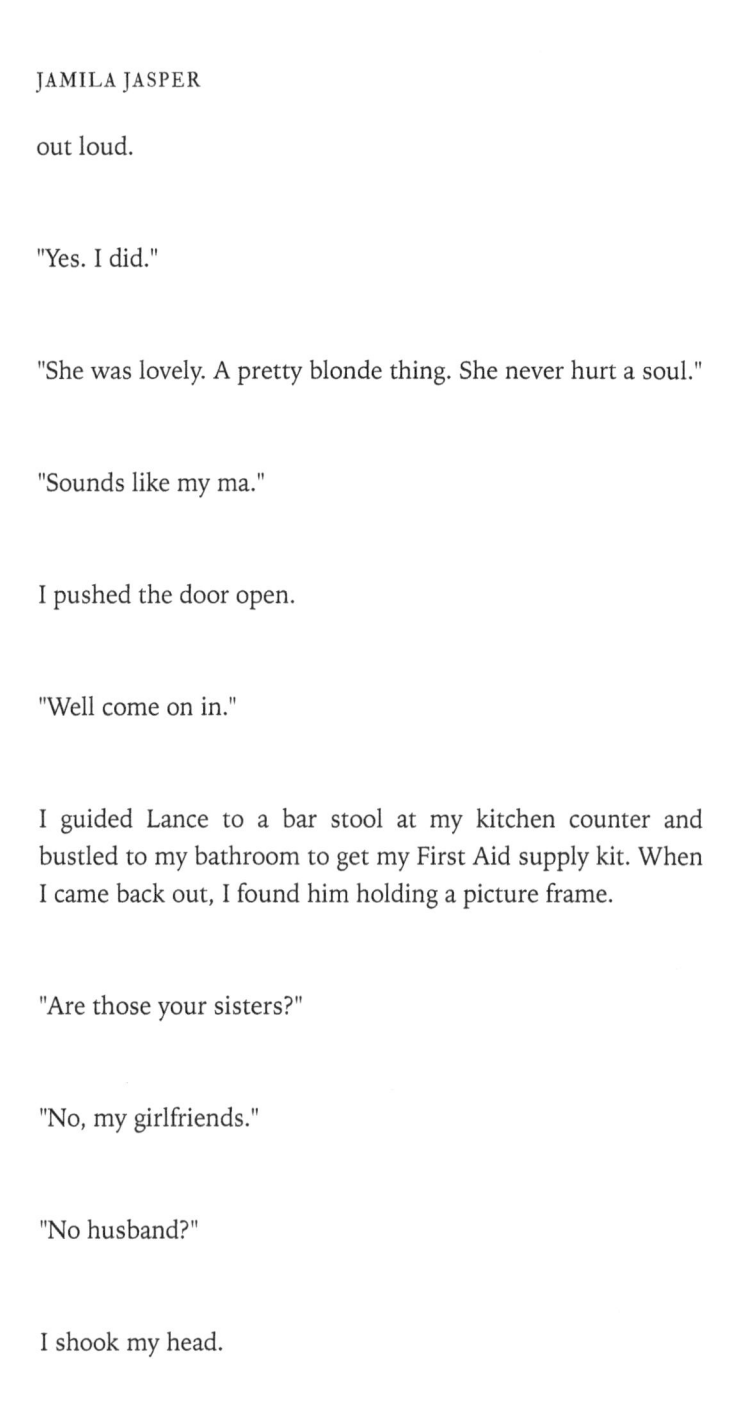

"Yes. I did."

"She was lovely. A pretty blonde thing. She never hurt a soul."

"Sounds like my ma."

I pushed the door open.

"Well come on in."

I guided Lance to a bar stool at my kitchen counter and bustled to my bathroom to get my First Aid supply kit. When I came back out, I found him holding a picture frame.

"Are those your sisters?"

"No, my girlfriends."

"No husband?"

I shook my head.

"Really?"

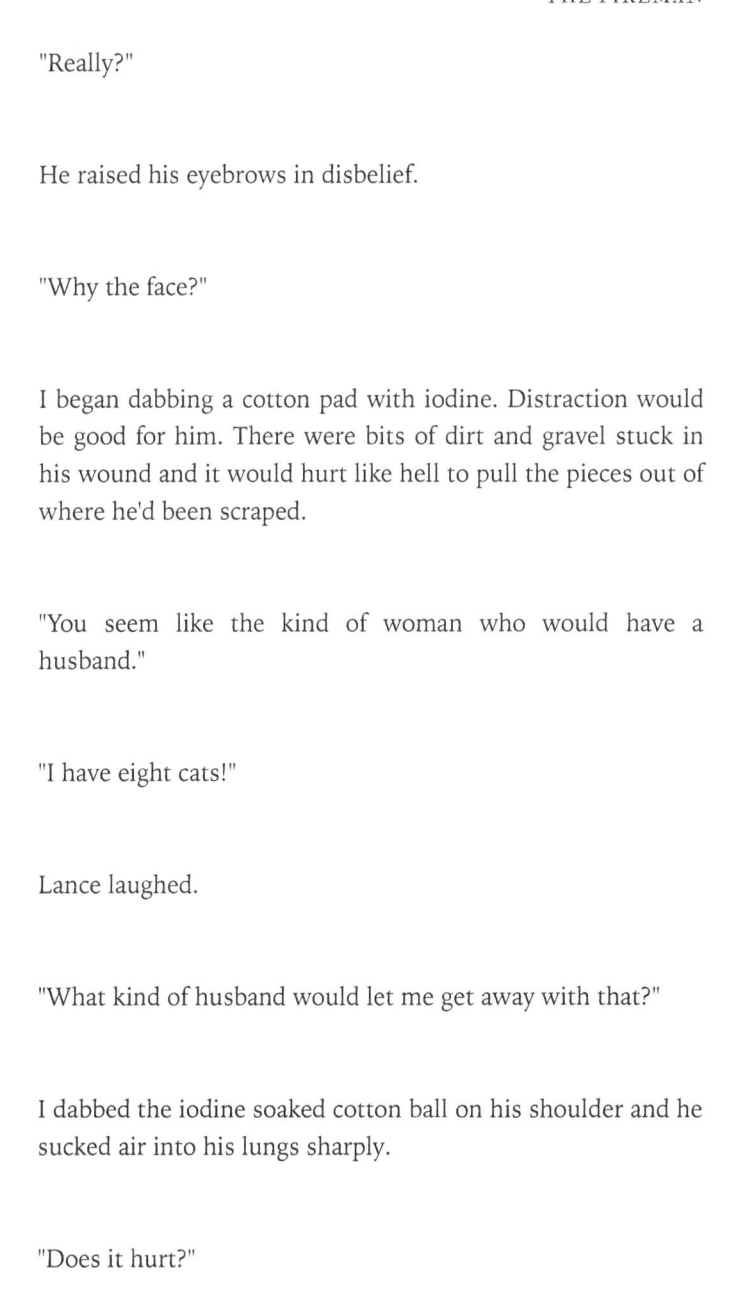

He raised his eyebrows in disbelief.

"Why the face?"

I began dabbing a cotton pad with iodine. Distraction would be good for him. There were bits of dirt and gravel stuck in his wound and it would hurt like hell to pull the pieces out of where he'd been scraped.

"You seem like the kind of woman who would have a husband."

"I have eight cats!"

Lance laughed.

"What kind of husband would let me get away with that?"

I dabbed the iodine soaked cotton ball on his shoulder and he sucked air into his lungs sharply.

"Does it hurt?"

"No, not really."

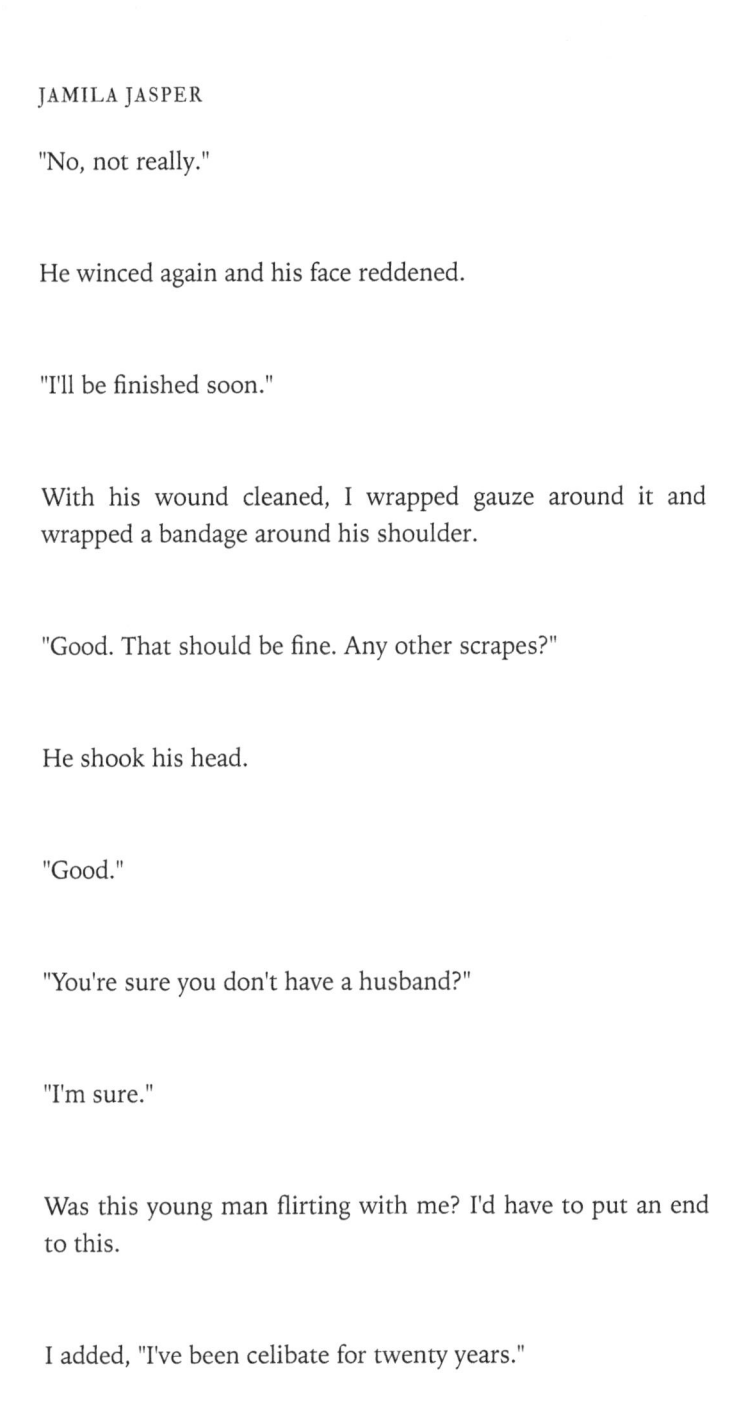

He winced again and his face reddened.

"I'll be finished soon."

With his wound cleaned, I wrapped gauze around it and wrapped a bandage around his shoulder.

"Good. That should be fine. Any other scrapes?"

He shook his head.

"Good."

"You're sure you don't have a husband?"

"I'm sure."

Was this young man flirting with me? I'd have to put an end to this.

I added, "I've been celibate for twenty years."

"Woah."

I smirked. Again, he seemed surprised. Telling most men about my two-decade-long vow of celibacy never failed to scare them off.

"Was that supposed to scare me?"

My mouth hung open.

"What the hell does that mean?"

"I mean, I can only think of one reason why you would mention your vow of celibacy. You're trying to scare me."

He stood, all 6'5" of him towering over me.

"What are you getting at?"

"I know your type... You think by telling me you're celibate, I won't pursue you."

"Pursue me? Who said anything about pursuing me?"

He grinned, "I did. Right now. I'm interested in pursuing you. Is that a problem?"

"N-no. I'm not looking for anyone!"

"Yeah right. I saw the way you looked at me. I saw that filthy hot desire burning in your eyes. You can deny it Zelda, but I won't believe you."

"You're crazy!"

"If I'm crazy, why haven't you kicked me out of your house yet? Why haven't you told me to get on my way and to leave you the hell alone?"

I stammered and then frustrated I threw my hands up in defeat.

"Get out then!"

"You're not serious..."

He stepped closer to me, his musk emanating from his flesh, the warm flesh I'd just touched and bandaged and nearly healed.

"No... I... I... Thank you for saving Homer!" I blurted out.

He grinned.

"No problem. Now, Miss Zelda, I told you I'm pursuing you. And I need an answer now. I can't wait. Are you down, or not?"

Younger men had grown a lot bolder since my younger days! This thirty-five-year-old walked up into my house like he owned the place and in a few minutes flat he'd not only made his intentions clear but he'd put pressure on me to make my mind up. 20 years of celibacy flashed before my eyes in an instant. In those two decades, not a single man had ever been that up front with me. That was all I'd wanted. That was all I'd ever been waiting for.

"Yes," I replied breathily, "I'm down."

"Perfect."

"But it's been twenty years!"

"So what? It doesn't close down. Trust me Zelda, I'll make it worth your while. I've fantasized about a woman like you for a long time..."

A woman like me? What did that mean? Lance didn't give me time to question what he meant. He didn't give me occasion to turn him down either. He swooped in and scooped me off my feet. I squealed as he spread my thighs apart and pressed me against the wall, kissing me furiously.

"Ohhh!"

He effortlessly supported my hips and thighs as he worked his hands up my dress, savoring the touch of my flesh with his palms as his lips traveled all over my neck and down my collar bone. I'd been left to my fantasies for so long that a man's mere touch instantly dampened the space between my thighs.

I whimpered as he pushed my panties to the side and without hesitation, thrust his fingers between my legs into my sopping wetness.

"OHHH!" I screamed louder.

Lance smirked and began to pump his fingers in and out of my tight hole. I cried out as my wetness clamped hard around his fingers. I let out a squeal as I came...

That had been incredible. In a few short seconds, I'd gone from warmed up to blazing hot. I couldn't wait for more... Lance's fingers hadn't been enough. I grew ravenous with my desire for him which seemed to mount faster than it had for any man.

After a twenty year hiatus, I would break my fast and immediately succumb to the desires of this dominant man decades my junior. I couldn't have been more invigorated. Heat throbbed in my chest as my heart attempted to escape from my ribcage. My eyes glowed hot with desire and I reached forward for his cock, gripping the hard member through his jeans.

"Take those off young man," I ordered.

He moved my hand away.

"I make the rules around here. You might be bossy but remember, I'm the boss."

He turned me around and pressed my stomach up against the wall, hiking my skirt up as his lips wrapped around the flesh on my neck and sucked hard. I moaned as he pulled my flesh into his mouth, sending shooting jolts of pain and pleasure surging through my spine.

Instead of removing his cock from his pants, he got down on his knees. He slipped my panties off over my hips and waist, exposing my full trimmed bush.

"Daddy can't wait to taste you..." he growled.

Our interaction had escalated so quickly that I wondered if he'd planned this all along. Or maybe Turtle had... Either way, I wasn't complaining.

He spread my thighs apart for his pleasure and darted his tongue between my legs. He lapped carelessly around my folds, surprising my flesh with ever touch of his warm tongue. Pressed against the wall, heat rushed to my cheeks and I cried out in pleasure each time his tongue darted deep beneath my folds and stroked my clit.

After licking my wetness, he stroked his tongue all the way back until it touched my tender, forbidden hole.

"OHHH!" I cried out.

Unfazed by my response, Lance grabbed my thighs and continued, tasting my forbidden backdoor until I moaned and bucked my hips from the force of orgasmic pleasure that surged through me.

I came so hard that my juices dripped down my thighs. Lance lapped up every last drop of my juices and then got to his feet, ready to take me from behind.

"I hope you're ready for this..." he murmured.

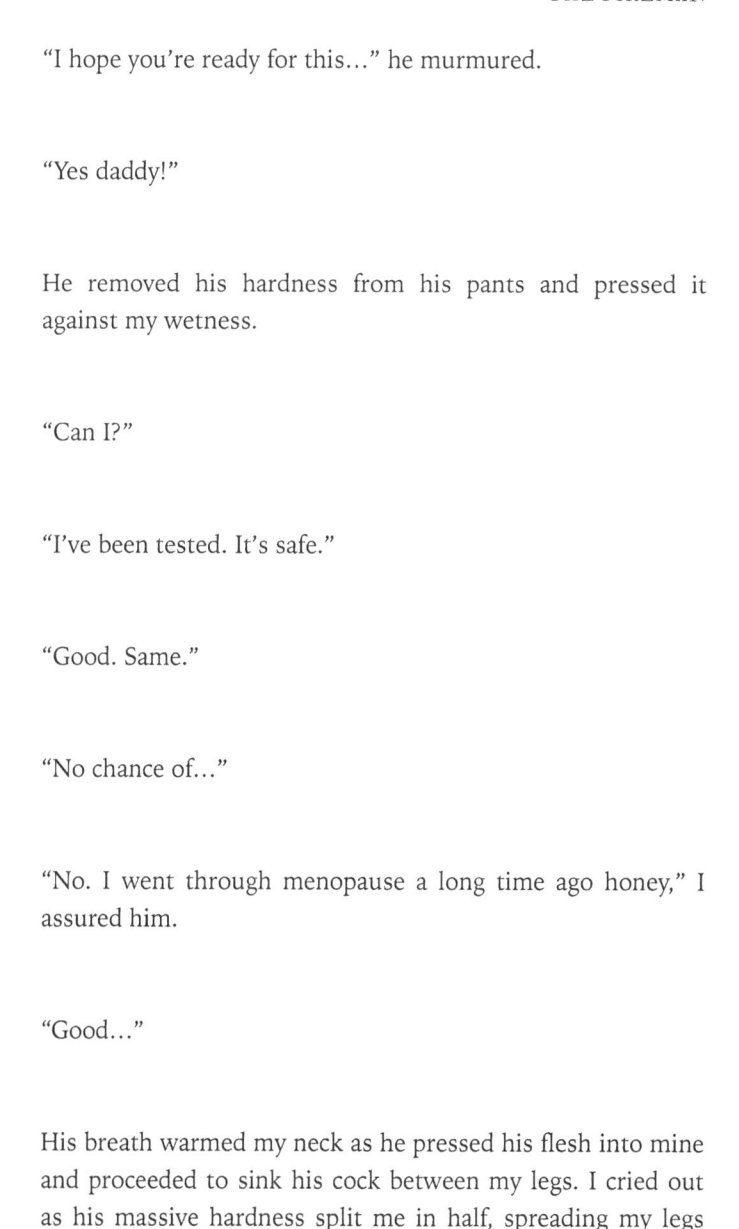

"Yes daddy!"

He removed his hardness from his pants and pressed it against my wetness.

"Can I?"

"I've been tested. It's safe."

"Good. Same."

"No chance of..."

"No. I went through menopause a long time ago honey," I assured him.

"Good..."

His breath warmed my neck as he pressed his flesh into mine and proceeded to sink his cock between my legs. I cried out as his massive hardness split me in half, spreading my legs further apart as he shoved every inch inside of me.

I slammed my palms into the wall and jutted my hips back to meet his thrusting as he pressed over ten inches of thick throbbing cock between my legs. I whimpered as he started to pump into me harder.

"Yes! Yes Lance!!!"

I moaned louder and louder as he thrust into me harder and faster. We both worked up a quick sweat, appropriate for a sweltering hot summer day. I cried out as he drove into me deeper and gripped my hips to allow him better access to my drooling pussy.

He pumped into me again and again until I came with explosive force. I cried out as my juices squirted all over his wetness and dripped down my thighs. Lance grunted as he kept thrusting into me harder and harder. It wouldn't be long until this powerful fireman reached a climax of his own.

"Don't stop!" I whimpered.

He groaned and thrust into me deeper, delivering more pleasure than I could have ever expected directly to my core. I exploded in another climax and even more of my creamy juices coated his thick veiny cock.

Lance couldn't hold back any longer and he groaned as he erupted, spurting thick rivers of cum between my legs. I gasped as my hair stuck to my forehead and my dress stuck to my thighs from the mixture of sweat and our combined juices. He left his thick cock inside me until every last drop of his cum entered my wetness.

When he pulled away from me, he turned me around and kissed me on the lips right away.

"This time tomorrow, I'll be back for more. I've got another job to take care of."

Before I could stop him, my nasty, filthy fireman dressed and walked out the front door. I should have been shaken, shocked and maybe even disgusted but to tell you the truth? I wasn't. I couldn't wait for him to come back the next day and give me more of what I desperately wanted… a hot young stud with the stamina of ten thousand men.

I fixed my dress and made myself another glass of iced tea. I picked up Homer and took him to sit on my lap in the living room as I reached for the phone. I *had* to call Ronice and tell her exactly what had happened to me. I didn't know if she'd believe me, but I had to tell someone.

Otherwise, this might as well have been a dream.

The End.

2

FREE SAMPLE: THE BUILDER

My head felt like it was on the verge of busting open.

The sound of power tools outside was proving a constant distraction to my work, which was already going poorly enough as it was. I'd thought, by taking my papers home from the university and grading them in the privacy of my own study, I might actually manage to get something done. My students had this irritating habit of totally disregarding my office hours, and swinging by just whenever they happened to need something, making it next to impossible for me to accomplish anything.

A woman professor not receiving the respect she deserves from her students? Shocking, I know.

Although it was really more just a matter of being a woman, period. As a Gender Studies professor for the past twenty-five years, nothing should have surprised me at this point. And it's true, I'd made significant headway over the years, and I would argue that the cause of feminism has never been stronger than it is today. Still, though, when you're actually dealing with the day to day bullshit as just about any working woman can tell you, the notion of genuine progress starts to feel less and less defined.

I can't even begin to tell you what a common thing it was for men to simply look right through me. Both my students, as well as my colleagues. Red-blooded males in their late teens and early twenties who found themselves forced into my classes as electives, spending the whole time talking and flirting, distracting the other students, and refusing to take me seriously whenever I called them out on it. Other professors who would talk right over me at faculty meetings, interrupting me mid-sentence. And the list goes on and on.

I don't even want to get into my ex-husband, a sociology professor who impressed me with his seemingly well-intentioned feminist ideals, but then spent an entire year cheating on me behind my back with not one, but two of this young female students. Somehow, he managed to hold onto his job after all that, and perhaps predictably, his standing actually improved among our colleagues once the two of us split, while I was humiliated and made to feel like some sort of social pariah for the next several months.

And I know I might sound bitter about all of this, but frankly, I have good reason to be. My girl friends were my only source of hope: Shontal, Tasha, Kishawn and even Zelda. Zelda and Kishawn kept me strong in my faith while Tasha and Shontal were known for walking on the wild-side and always encouraged me to get out of my shell and relax more.

How could I relax?

Over twenty-five years, I'd watched the cause of gender equality give the appearance of improving by leaps and bounds, but as far as what was going on right under my nose, it was beginning to feel more and more like a lost cause with each day that passes.

I supposed I could be considered a success as far as that goes. There was some consolation in knowing that I'd changed at least a few young women's lives for the better, inspired them in their careers, or at the very least, helped them to recognize their own self-worth. And even if that hadn't been the case, even if I'd spent all that time simply spouting hot air, only to have it fall on deaf ears, I'd at least done well by myself as far as a career went. I mean, if I hadn't been successful, I wouldn't be sitting here in my cozy colonial home, sitting back in a leather desk chair with a glass of scotch at hand. And I certainly wouldn't be able to afford the renovations I'd been paying out the wazoo for over the past several months.

Those renovations, incidentally, being a significant player in my present distractions.

I'd been facing away from the window until now, but presently I turned to open up the curtains, giving up all pretense of successfully grading the papers I had at hand.

A shiver ran through my body as I caught sight of the man outside in my backyard, steadily at work on the construction of a gazebo. Derek was his name. He was already a tempting enough distraction as it was- tall, bulky with muscle, a light film of stubble across his chin. But to make matters even worse, he'd since taken off his shirt in the setting summer sun. Now, as he leaned and strained and shuffled building materials around through my backyard, I was treated to an absolute visual smorgasbord. I found myself utterly entranced by the play of the golden light against his straining musculature. His back rippling, his arms pulsing, rivulets of sweat glistening as they poured along his broad, heaving chest, his six-pack abs, and slid down along the maddeningly entrenched V-lines of his Adonis' muscles.

It didn't take me long at all to go from annoyed leering to outright ogling my delectable little construction worker, and I felt a familiar stirring between my legs as I watched him, one that hadn't properly been satisfied in years.

THE FIREMAN

I watched as he bent over, the top of his jeans sliding down along his backside, the crack of his ass peeking just into view, as well as the very tops of two tight, highly sculpted cheeks.

My breath caught in my throat.

I felt like a teenager all of the sudden, an adolescent lust awakened in me that threatened to overpower me. I knew it was absurd, but I couldn't look away. I nearly licked my lips at him, and secretly wished that those jeans would inch down just a little bit further, and further, and then slide the rest of the way down while they were at it.

Then, without warning, he reached back and hiked them back up again. His body began to turn, seeming to move in my direction, and I panicked.

I grabbed the curtains and yanked them tightly shut so that barely a sliver of outside light was permitted to seep into the room.

I leaned against the wall, breathless, shaking, trying to understand my overreaction to this whole situation.

At first, it was a kind of moral indignation against myself. I was objectifying this man the way I spent my days rallying against men doing to women. Seeing him like a cut of meat hanging in a butcher's shop, rather than as a human being (although, to be fair, if you'd have seen him, I could hardly be faulted for that...)

>END OF SAMPLE<

Finish book: mybook.to/TheBuilder

AFTERWORD

Dear Reader,

Thank you so much for reading my book.

For making it all the way to the end of this book, I want to offer you a **FREE gift**.

This offer is exclusively for readers:

Sign up to my newsletter and receive **3 FREE BWWM romance novels** just like this one, as well as a **FREE BWWM romance audiobook**.

If you LOVE reading romance and you want instant access to more FREE books, click the link below.

Click here to sign up: http://bit.ly/jamilajasper
Enjoy the freebies!
Jamila

MORE JAMILA JASPER ROMANCE

Keep reading past this section to find out how to get Jamila Jasper books for FREE!

FULL CATALOG BY JAMILA JASPER:

http://jamilajasperromance.com/2018/05/07/complete-amazon-back-catalog-jamila-jasper-bwwm-romance-author/

NON-EXCLUSIVE INTERRACIAL ROMANCE TITLES:

http://jamilajasperromance.com/2018/01/12/nook-kobo-ibooks-google-play-bwwm-book-list-published-wide-interracial-romance/

JAMILA JASPER ROMANCE AUDIOBOOK COLLECTION:

http://jamilajasperromance.com/2018/01/12/bwwm-romance-on-audio-book-jamila-jasper-interracial-romance-audio-collection/

PATREON

EVEN MORE BONUS CONTENT FOR LESS THAN $2/MONTH:

I've just launched a new opportunity for you to get a "backstage pass" to Jamila Jasper publishing by joining my Patreon!

For a small monthly fee, you get exclusive access to materials NOT available on my mailing list.

You'll receive:

Free short story audiobooks and audiobook samples when they're ready

#FirstDraftLeaks of Prologues and first chapters **weeks** before I hit publish

Notes from Jamila -- blog posts from my writing desk about my process so you can get to know the writer better

Click here to join: www.patreon.com/jamilajasper

Gold Subscribers, Platinum Subscribers, (and more) get more exclusive content: you can get characters named after you, a mention in my dedication and even participate in deciding KEY aspects of the plot.

PATREON

Check out the tiered subscription plans starting at $1.49/month, less than your daily morning coffee!

Click here: www.patreon.com/jamilajasper

SOCIAL MEDIA

Join me on social media! You'll find a reasonable number of daily posts, personal interaction & a welcoming community of interracial romance readers:

www.instagram.com/bwwmjamila
  www.twitter.com/jamilajasper
  www.facebook.com/bwwmjamila
   jamilajasperromance@gmail.com
   www.jamilajasperromance.com

ACKNOWLEDGMENTS

Thank you to all my readers for joining me on this journey. I love writing "fun" stories to break up the longer novels and this series has been stewing in my head for a long time. We love us some billionaires, some bad boys and mafiosos too but sometimes these regular guys can be FINE as heck too! I wanted to give 'em a chance and give US a chance to indulge in some of our finer fantasies… What do you think?

CPSIA information can be obtained
at www.ICGtesting.com
Printed in the USA
LVHW111611110822
725707LV00003B/378